Dear Henry and Kate,

    You always loved my cooking and especially my Saturday morning pancakes. Remember the time when I flipped a pancake right onto Henry's head and he ate it anyway?

    Well, I thought it'd be fun if I put together this collection of recipes for you that I brought back from Chewandswallow.

    Your mom and I are here to help. So, let's cook up a storm.

Love 'n' hugs,
GRANDPA

atheneum

ATHENEUM BOOKS FOR YOUNG READERS
An imprint of Simon & Schuster Children's Publishing Division
1230 Avenue of the Americas, New York, New York 10020
Text copyright © 2013 by Judi Barrett
Illustrations copyright © 2013 by Ronald Barrett
Special thanks to food stylist Ashley Ristau, photographer Raymond Hom, and prop stylist Michelle Wong
Book indexed by Edwina Walker Amorosa
For information about special discounts for bulk purchases, please contact Simon & Schuster Special Sales
at 1-866-506-1949 or business@simonandschuster.com.
The Simon & Schuster Speakers Bureau can bring authors to your live event. For more information or to book an event,
contact the Simon & Schuster Speakers Bureau at 1-866-248-3049 or visit our website at www.simonspeakers.com.
Book design by Lauren Rille and Jane Archer
The text for this book is set in ITC Cheltenham Std.
The illustrations for this book are rendered in tomato sauce.
Manufactured in China
0613 SCP
First Edition
10 9 8 7 6 5 4 3 2 1
Library of Congress Cataloging-in-Publication Data
Barrett, Judi.
Grandpa's cloudy with a chance of meatballs cookbook / Judi Barrett ; illustrated by Ron Barrett. — 1st ed.
p.   cm.
Audience: 4–8.
Audience: K to grade 3.
ISBN 978-1-4424-4475-1
ISBN 978-1-4424-4476-8 (eBook)
1. Cooking—Juvenile literature. I. Barrett, Ron, ill. II. Title.
TX652.5.B254 2013
641.5—dc23   2012045731

Grandpa's Cloudy With a Chance of Meatballs Cookbook

Written by Judi Barrett

Drawn by Ron Barrett

atheneum

Atheneum Books for Young Readers

NEW YORK LONDON TORONTO SYDNEY NEW DELHI

Grandpa's Rules and Tools

Ready! Set! Cook!

Cook up a storm and have a good time doing it! And don't forget to chew and swallow!

- Wear an apron.

- Roll up your sleeves (if you have them).

- Always wash your hands with soap and warm water, and dry them.

- Tie your hair back if it's long enough to get in your way.

- Always have a grown-up in the kitchen to show you how to do things and to help you if you need it.

- Read the recipe first, so you'll know what ingredients you'll need.

- Review the directions carefully, so you'll understand what you have to do.

- Wash and dry all fruits and veggies.

- Be careful when turning on the stove. Always let an adult help you.

- Only heat the stove to the temperature the recipe calls for. Otherwise you'll have undercooked or overcooked food!

- Stir what's in the pot slowly and carefully. That way you, the stove, and the walls won't get splattered.

- Stoves get HOT!

- Pots get HOT!

- With help from an adult, always cut slowly and carefully with a knife. Always cut away from you, and watch those fingers. You want to have ten when you're finished cooking!

- Use pot holders when removing anything from the oven and when picking up hot pots or pot lids.

- Measure your ingredients carefully.

- It helps if you clean up as you go along, but be sure to *really* clean up afterward!!!

Contents

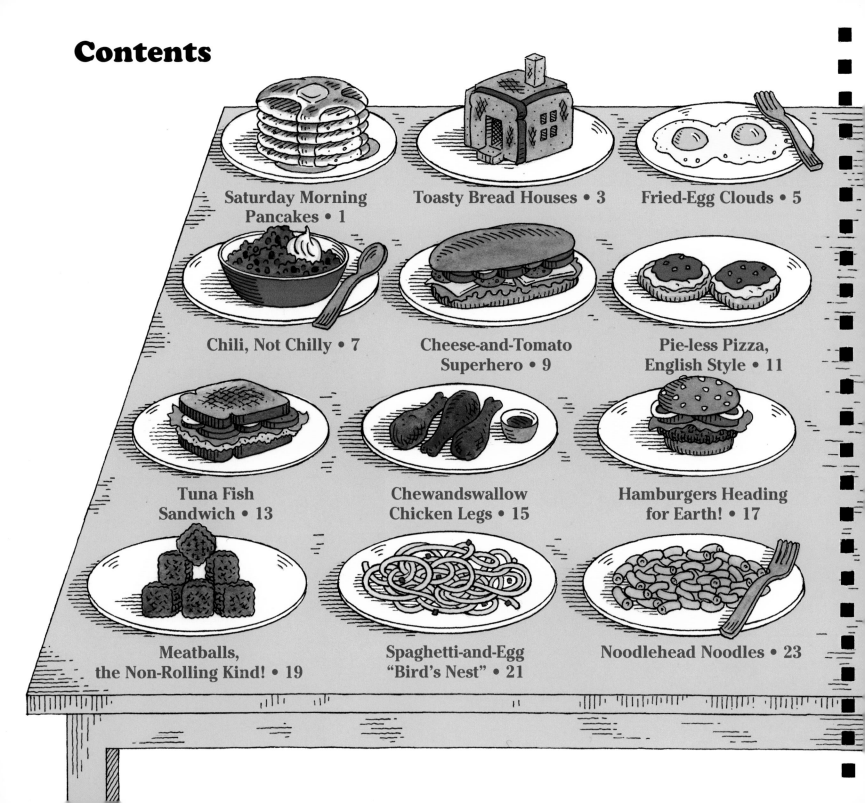

Saturday Morning Pancakes

Make them on Sunday, Monday, Tuesday, Wednesday, Thursday, or Friday mornings too! And try to avoid flipping them onto anyone's head!

Ingredients *yields 8 pancakes*

- ½ cup whole wheat flour
- ½ cup all-purpose flour
- 1 tablespoon sugar
- 1 teaspoon baking powder
- ½ teaspoon baking soda
- Pinch of salt
- 1 egg
- 1 cup buttermilk
- Handful of blueberries (optional)
- 3 tablespoons melted margarine or butter

Directions

1 In a large bowl, combine the flours, sugar, baking powder, baking soda, and salt. Stir.

2 Using a wire whisk, add the egg and buttermilk and mix until smooth. If desired, add the blueberries now. Stir in the melted butter.

3 Heat a nonstick skillet over medium heat. Pour ¼ cup of batter onto the skillet for each pancake. When it's golden brown and little holes appear on the surface, flip it *very carefully* so the other side can turn golden. Aim for the pan, not for anyone's head!

Morning pancakes can also be afternoon pancakes or evening pancakes. Flip 'em and eat 'em!

YOU'LL FLIP OVER THEM!

Toasty Bread Houses

When the people of Chewandswallow moved to a new land, they made houses out of their toast rafts. Here's how you can build homes you can eat.

Ingredients *yields 2 houses*

- 12 or more slices of square bread, well toasted, with left and right crusts trimmed
- Nut butter, any kind (Allergic to nuts? Use SunButter.)

TOAST OF THE TOWN!

Directions

1 For each house, start with 4 slices, 1 slice for each side of the house. Have an adult help you cut out shapes for windows and a door.

2 With a butter knife or spatula, spread nut butter (or SunButter) on the side crusts of the toast. Stick the 4 slices together, edge to edge, so you form a box.

3 "Glue" on one more piece of toast for the roof. You can even add a chimney.

4 You can make up your own house shapes. Add a garage. Build an A-frame. Make a two-story house. Add a porch. (You'll need more toast!)

5 You can even make a doghouse for a very small dog!

Now munch away on your tasty, toasty houses!

Fried-Egg Clouds

Fry 'em up in a pan! No matter what the weather is like outside, the yolks will make your day sunny!

Ingredients *yields 1 serving*

- 2 large eggs
- 1½ tablespoons vegetable oil, margarine, or butter
- Salt and pepper to taste

I LIKE TO FLY IN A FRIED-EGG SKY!

Directions

1 Crack the eggs into a small bowl or plate, making sure the yolks don't break.

2 Place a frying pan over medium heat. Add the oil, margarine, or butter, let it melt, and swirl it around gently so it coats the pan.

3 Place or slide each egg into the pan.

Enjoy your delicious indoor clouds!

4 Fry them for about 2 to 2½ minutes. You can flip them "over easy" after around a minute. If you don't flip them, they're called sunny-side-up eggs.

5 Remove the pan from the heat when eggs are done. The yolks should wiggle. Add salt and pepper to taste.

6 Serve eggs on a plate, preferably a *sky blue* one.

6

Chili, Not Chilly

It'll definitely warm you up.

Ingredients *yields 4–6 servings*

- 2 tablespoons olive oil
- 1 onion, chopped
- 1 clove garlic, chopped fine
- 1 red pepper, chopped
- 2 to 3 tablespoons chili powder
- 1 1-pound package ground lean turkey
- ½ cup golden raisins
- 1 large 28-ounce can peeled whole Italian tomatoes
- Salt and pepper to taste

- 1 15-ounce can cannellini or black beans, drained and rinsed
- Dollop sour cream (optional)

GREAT BOWLS OF FIRE!

Directions

1 In a large heavy pot, add olive oil and then sauté the onion, garlic, red pepper, and 1 tablespoon of the chili powder. Cook over medium heat till veggies are soft, not crunchy (about 7 to 9 minutes)!

2 Add the turkey and, with a wooden spoon, break it up so it's not chunky. Add the rest of the chili powder and sauté till the turkey is no longer pink (about 5 minutes).

3 Add raisins, tomatoes and liquid (squished up with your fingers), salt and pepper, and the beans. Stir. Use a wooden spoon to further break up the tomatoes.

4 Bring to a boil, then simmer for 40 to 45 minutes, partially covered. You may want to use a splatter screen on the pot to prevent red dots from getting all over your stove.

5 Fill your bowl and add a dollop of sour cream.

6 It tastes even better the next day!

Chill out and enjoy your chili that's not from Chile!

Cheese-and-Tomato Superhero

Here are two kinds of superheroes. One's a long tasty sandwich that you can make in your kitchen and one's a very special person named Grandpa.

Ingredients *yields 4–6 servings*

- 1 loaf Italian or French long bread (about 6 inches), split lengthwise
- Olive oil and red wine vinegar to taste
- 1 small tomato, sliced
- 3 slices of cheese (your choice)
- Italian salami and/or prosciutto, sliced (as much as you'd like)
- 2 leaves of lettuce
- Pickles, sliced
- Very thin onion slices
- Salt and pepper to taste

(Also known as a submarine [sub] sandwich, Italian sandwich, po'boy, hoagie, wedge, zep, bomber, torpedo, or grinder. Different names are used in different areas of the United States.)

Directions

1 Pull out some of the doughy inside part of the bread so more good stuff can fit into your sandwich.

2 Sprinkle a moderate amount of the oil and vinegar on the hollowed insides of the bread.

3 Fill bread with layers of tomato, cheese, salami and/or prosciutto, lettuce, pickles, onion, salt, and pepper.

4 Close sandwich. Lean on it a bit to flatten it slightly. Slice into manageable servings and *mangia*!!!!!

This is a "heroic" non-cooking experience. Enjoy your delectable Hero!

IT'S SUPPERMAN!

10

Pie-less Pizza, English Style

How can you make Italian pizza without making a pizza pie? By making an English muffin pizza!

Ingredients *yields 4 servings*

- 4 English muffins, split in halves
- 1 16-ounce jar of store-bought pizza sauce
- 1 8-ounce package of shredded mozzarella cheese
- About 1½ teaspoons of dried oregano
- About 1 tablespoon fresh basil, chopped (optional)

A MINI-MEAL FIT FOR A KING!

Directions

1 Cover a flat baking sheet with nonstick foil.

2 Toast the muffin halves in a toaster, so the sauce won't make them mushy. Set the oven to low broil. Lie each half on the baking sheet, with the nooks and crannies looking up at you.

3 Spoon pizza sauce (about 1 to 2 table-spoons) onto each muffin half and add shredded mozzarella (about 2 tablespoons). Add more pizza sauce (1 tablespoon) and sprinkle with oregano and basil.

Pizza *perfecto*. Fit for a queen!

4 Using pot holders, place the sheet under the broiler and watch it carefully! The cheese should melt and the muffins will brown—but don't cremate them. It should take 3 to 5 minutes.

5 When pizzas look done, take the pan (hot!) from the oven and put it on a surface that won't melt. Watch those tender fingers!

6 Use a spatula to place pizza halves on a plate, and serve to each hungry person. Watch the smiles appear and the pizzas disappear.

Tuna Fish Sandwich

Make a normal-size version of that gigantic sandwich for your lunch. This one doesn't need to be airlifted! Just lift it up and put it in your mouth.

Ingredients *yields 1 sandwich*

- 1 3-ounce can of tuna in water
- 1 medium celery stalk, diced
- 2 scallions, chopped fine
- 16 golden raisins
- Sprinkle of ground black pepper
- Pinch of salt
- 2 tablespoons light mayonnaise
- 2 slices whole wheat bread, lightly toasted
- 1 lettuce leaf, to fit
- 1 tomato slice (optional)
- 1 pickle (optional)

Directions

1 Open can of tuna *carefully* (watch your fingers!), drain liquid, and put in a medium bowl. Mash it up with a fork.

2 Add celery, scallions, raisins, pepper, salt, and mayo, and mush them all together.

3 Spread mixture onto one side of toast, add lettuce, tomato slice, and pickle, if desired, and top with the second piece of toast. Pat down gently.

4 Slice sandwich in half and put it on a plate carefully so it doesn't lose its insides.

5 You're ready for your tuna fish feast!

I CAUGHT ONE!

No helicopter needed. Just your appetite and a crispy pickle.

Chewandswallow Chicken Legs

Eat them no matter what the weather is outside. . . . Inside it's chicken legs!

Ingredients *yields 4 servings*

- 4 tablespoons olive oil
- 2 teaspoons of your favorite mustard
- Juice of 1 lemon
- Juice of ½ an orange
- 1 garlic clove, finely diced
- 1 teaspoon paprika
- Salt and pepper to taste
- 2 tablespoons honey
- 1 tablespoon balsamic vinegar
- 8 chicken legs (drumsticks)

LOTS OF CLUCK WITH THIS RECIPE!

Directions

1 In a large bowl, combine olive oil, mustard, lemon juice, orange juice, garlic, paprika, salt and pepper, honey, and balsamic vinegar, and whisk together well.

2 Wash chicken legs under water and dry off with paper towels. Then wash your hands *really* well, with soap, after touching the raw chicken!

3 Add the legs to the mixture and let it marinate in the fridge for 2 to 3 hours, covered.

4 Preheat oven to 375 degrees. Put the legs and 3 tablespoons of the marinade into a Pyrex pan. For the sauce, boil the rest of the marinade in a small pot on the stove till it's thickish (about 5 minutes).

5 Bake legs for 50 to 60 minutes, turning once halfway through. They're done when juices run clear when poked with a fork.

Grab one before it runs away!

Hamburgers Heading for Earth!

What could be more exciting than a burger from space making a spectacular landing right smack on your dinner plate?

Ingredients *yields 4 servings*

- 1 pound low-fat, lean ground sirloin
- 2 tablespoons ketchup
- 1 teaspoon garlic powder
- Dash of salt and pepper
- Squirt or two of Worcestershire sauce
- 4 hamburger buns

THEY'RE OUT OF THIS WORLD!

Directions

1 Squish the meat, ketchup, garlic powder, salt, pepper, and Worcestershire sauce together until they're all mixed up, but don't oversquish!

2 Divide the meat into four equal parts and then shape the patties into flat, ½-inch-thick circles.

3 Turn oven to broil. Put the patties in a broiler pan and sprinkle on a little extra garlic powder. Put the pan under the broiler and keep your eye on the patties as they get cooked and browned. Flip them once after about 5 minutes. They should take about 5 to 6 minutes on each side, give or take a minute or 2.

4 When they are done, remove the pan from the oven with a mitt and, using a flipper, place your burgers on a bun and land them on your plate.

5 You can add tomato slices, onion slices, pickles, lettuce, ketchup, mustard, even all of these . . . or you can just eat 'em plain.

A tasty Chewandswallow event right in your kitchen.

Meatballs, the Non-Rolling Kind!

They taste as good as the round ones, but they can't roll off your plate.

Ingredients *yields 5–6 servings*

- 1 pound lean ground sirloin
- 1 piece of multigrain bread
- 3 tablespoons milk
- 2 tablespoons plus ¾ cup breadcrumbs
- 2 tablespoons ketchup
- 1 teaspoon garlic powder
- 1 tablespoon chopped parsley
- Salt and pepper to taste
- 5 tablespoons olive oil

They'll stay wherever you put them, especially if you put them in your mouth!

IT'S A CUBIST WORLD, AFTER ALL!

Directions

1 Put the meat in a large bowl.

2 Put the bread in a small bowl, add milk, and soak for 10 minutes. Squeeze and crumble the bread onto the meat.

3 Add 2 tablespoons of the breadcrumbs, and the ketchup, garlic powder, parsley, and salt and pepper to the meat.

4 Squish it all together with both *(clean)* hands but don't oversquish—just till it stays in a solid shape.

Cloudy with a chance of meatcubes!

5 Tear off a clump of meat, roll into a 1-inch ball, and then, using your hands, flatten it so it has 6 sides, like a cube. Keep making meatcubes. You should end up with about 20.

6 Dip meatcubes in the remaining breadcrumbs and set them aside.

7 Heat olive oil in a pan over medium heat and lightly brown all sides of the meatcubes, turning them with a small spatula. Cook for about 15 to 20 minutes, turning frequently so all sides get cooked.

Spaghetti-and-Egg "Bird's Nest"

It's not high up in a Chewandswallow tree but right there on your plate!

Ingredients *yields 4–6 servings*

- 2 teaspoons olive oil or butter
- 1 clove garlic, diced
- Leftover cold, cooked spaghetti (a good handful-size portion)
- 2 large eggs, beaten
- 2–3 leaves fresh basil, chopped fine
- Dash of salt and pepper

IT'S FOR THE BIRDS AND FOR YOU!

Directions

1 In a medium-size saucepan on low heat, add olive oil or butter, and garlic. Sauté till garlic is yellowish, but not brown—about 1 to 2 minutes.

2 Raise heat a bit. Add spaghetti and stir it around in the oil until it's coated. Flatten it out with a spatula and sauté it so it's not fried but on its way to being sort of crunchy—about 5 to 7 minutes.

3 Spill the beaten eggs and basil onto the top of the spaghetti and mix it to spread the eggs around. Add salt and pepper.

4 Cook it until the eggs and spaghetti form a solid fried mass (about 2 to 3 minutes)—a nice, flat bird's nest. Flip the nest to finish cooking the egg—about 1 minute.

5 Slide it onto a plate and divide it into people-size portions.

Eat it before a bird calls it home.

Noodlehead Noodles

Create this yummy mixture of cheese and pasta. Put it in a bowl (not on your head) and eat it!

Ingredients *yields 4–6 servings*

- 2 cups uncooked macaroni (spinach, whole wheat—whatever you'd like!)
- ¾ cup whole or low-fat milk
- 4 slices cheddar or American cheese
- 1 tablespoon butter or margarine
- Pinch of paprika
- 1 tablespoon grated parmesan cheese
- Salt and pepper to taste

IT'S ANOTHER KIND OF MAC ATTACK!

Directions

1 Fill a medium pot with water and bring to a boil. Add macaroni. Boil according to package instructions or until pasta is chewy, not mushy. Test by fishing for one with a slotted spoon. Be careful, they're hot!

2 Drain macaroni in a colander in the sink.

3 In a nonstick pot, add milk, sliced cheese, and butter or margarine, and cook on very low heat, whisking until cheese is melted. Add paprika and parmesan cheese.

4 Put cooked macaroni in serving bowl. Add cheese mixture and stir.

Use your "noodle" and eat your noodles.

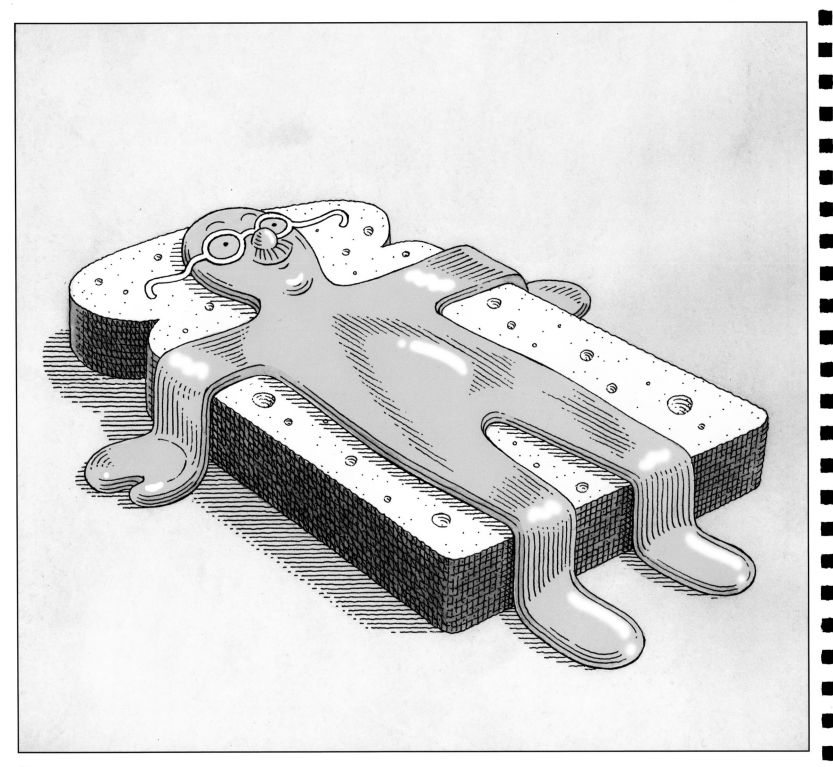

Grilled Cheese Sandwich

This gooey, toasty, tasty, and lip-smackin' good sandwich is recommended by "The Big Cheese" himself.

Ingredients *yields 1 serving*

- 1 slice of bread (your choice)
- 1 slice of cheese, any variety
- Mustard (optional)

IT'S LOVED BY BOYS AND GRILLS!

Directions

1 Take a slice of your favorite bread and put it on a baking pan that is lined with non-stick foil.

2 Place 1 slice of cheese on the bread.

3 Turn the oven to broil and put the pan into the oven. Leave the door slightly open and keep a sharp eye on the melting process.

4 When the cheese has melted and bubbled a bit—but not burned (it can happen very quickly)—take the pan out using pot holders.

5 Put the pan down on a heat-proof surface. Use a metal spatula to remove the bread from the pan and serve. Wait a moment before eating because it will be very hot!!!!!

6 Enjoy your 1-piece-of-bread "sandwich." (This is called an open-faced sandwich.) You can dip it in mustard for a tangy treat!

Smile and say "CHEESE!"

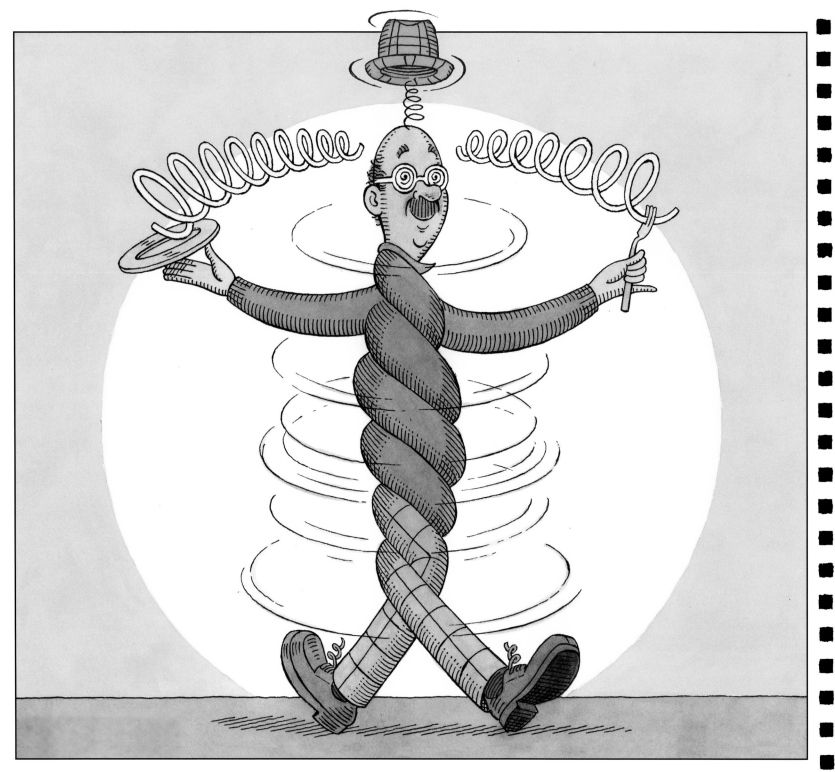

Spaghetti Twister with a Tomato Tornado

Here's some deliciously stormy weather you can eat.
Watch out! Take shelter in your kitchen and cook up a storm.

Ingredients *yields 4–6 servings*

- 1 medium onion, chopped fine
- 2 cloves garlic, chopped fine
- 4 leaves basil and 3 sprigs parsley, chopped
- 3 tablespoons olive oil
- 1 28-ounce can peeled whole Italian tomatoes
- 1 tablespoon tomato paste
- Salt and pepper to taste
- 1 box spaghetti (spinach, whole wheat, multigrain, etc.)
- 1 tablespoon grated parmesan cheese

Directions

1 In a pot, sauté the onion, garlic, basil, and parsley in olive oil, stirring here and there, until onions are golden—around 15 minutes.

2 Put tomatoes into a blender, and pulse it into a tomato tornado (you want some lumps left).

3 Add the tomatoes, paste, salt, and pepper to the onion mixture and cook on low, uncovered, for 35 minutes. Stir occasionally.

4 Cook spaghetti according to package directions.

5 Using pot holders, have an adult pour the spaghetti into a colander in the sink to drain. Serve spaghetti in bowls and top with tomato sauce and a sprinkling of parmesan cheese.

Twist the spaghetti around your fork and eat it with your tomato tornado!

I'M THE PASTA TWISTER!

27

28

Foggy Pea Soup

What better day could there be to make pea soup than on a foggy day? Hard to see out there, easy to see in your kitchen! So let's make a soup in honor of Chewandswallow weather.

Ingredients *yields 4 servings*

- 1 10-ounce bag frozen sweet green peas
- 2 cups low-sodium chicken broth
- ½ cup fresh parsley
- Salt and pepper to taste
- 6–7 leaves of Boston or Bibb lettuce
- ½ cup half-and-half

PEA-KA-BOO!

Directions

1 Cook peas according to package instructions.

2 In a blender, add the broth, parsley, salt, pepper, lettuce, and cooked peas. Puree.

3 Put the pureed mixture into a pot and simmer 10 minutes. Then add the half-and-half, stir, and ladle into bowls.

4 If serving cold, chill in the refrigerator. Then serve.

What did you find in the fog? Hopefully the bottom of your bowl!

French Un-Fries

Délicieuse, *crunchy, tasty, and healthy.*

Ingredients *yields 1–2 servings*

- 2 russet potatoes, scrubbed and rinsed, skins on
- 3 tablespoons olive oil
- 2 teaspoons garlic powder
- 2 teaspoons paprika
- 1 teaspoon oregano
- Salt and pepper to taste

WHAT'S NEXT? FRENCH UN-TOAST?

Directions

1 Preheat oven to 450 degrees.

2 Cut potatoes into long, skinny pieces—about 2 to 3 inches long.

3 In a large bowl, mix together the olive oil, garlic powder, paprika, oregano, salt, and pepper. Coat potatoes well with the mixture but not till they're dripping wet.

4 Spread potatoes out in a single layer onto a baking sheet covered in nonstick foil.

5 Bake for 25 to 35 minutes, turning occasionally.

Mange les pommes de terre!
Which means "Eat potatoes!"

Broccoli Tree Salad

Make a salad with broccoli trees, like the ones growing in Chewandswallow.

Ingredients *yields 4–6 servings*

- 2 tablespoons olive oil
- Juice of 1 lemon
- Salt and pepper to taste
- 1 clove garlic, sliced
- 1 head broccoli, cut up into lots of bite-size trees

WATCH OUT FOR SQUIRRELS IN YOUR SALAD!

Directions

1 In a serving bowl combine olive oil, lemon, salt, pepper, and garlic. Whisk together.

2 Wash broccoli trees and put into a pot with a steamer. Add enough water to just cover the steamer.

Eat your trees. They're good for you!

3 Boil, covered, until a fork can be easily inserted into the broccoli. Don't overcook!!!! Drain in colander.

4 Dump broccoli gently into the olive oil mixture and toss well.

5 Eat while warm—It tastes better.

34

Pickley Cucumbers

Are you in a pickle about what to eat with, or put on top of, your hamburger? Here's the perfect solution . . . homemade pickles!

Ingredients *yields 4–5 servings*

- 4–5 Kirby cucumbers
- 1 tablespoon salt
- ½ teaspoon sugar
- 1 tablespoon fresh dill, chopped
- 2 teaspoons cider vinegar
- Half a sweet Vidalia onion, thinly sliced
- 1 red pepper, chopped into little pieces

Directions

1 Wash cucumbers and slice really thinly—about ⅛ inch.

2 Put the cucumbers in a colander and sprinkle with salt. Place a small plate topped with a heavy weight in the colander and let it press down on them for 30 minutes. Liquid should drip out of the colander. That's good!

3 Remove the plate and weight. Rinse the salt off the cukes with cold water and squeeze them dry in a *clean* towel. You'll love the squeezing part, and they don't mind!

4 Put the cucumber slices into a bowl and toss with the sugar, dill, vinegar, sliced onion, and the chopped red pepper.

5 Refrigerate your pickley cukes and eat them either the same day or the very next day because they don't keep very well.

When you taste them you'll be just tickled!

THAT RHYMES WITH PICKLED!

Snowy Mashed Potatoes with Sunrise

Have a wintery scene on your plate in any season . . . a hill of warm, mushy, mashed potatoes, minus the sleds. Top it off with a buttery sun.

Ingredients *yields 4–6 servings*

- 6 medium russet potatoes, cut into 1-inch pieces
- ½ cup warm milk (whole or low fat)
- Pinch of salt
- Pinch of pepper
- 3 tablespoons butter or margarine

SHOVEL THEM IN!

Directions

1 You can peel the potatoes but they're healthier with their skins left on. Place the cut-up potatoes in a large pot and cover with cold water—about 1 inch over potatoes.

2 Bring to a boil. Lower the heat so it doesn't boil over and make a real mess. Cook for 25 to 30 minutes. You can tell if they're done by poking them with a fork. If it slides in and out easily, they're ready.

Winter doesn't taste better than this!

3 Using pot holders, pour potatoes and water carefully into a colander in the sink and let them drain.

4 Transfer the potatoes to a bowl. Add milk, salt, pepper, and 2 tablespoons of butter. Mash until most of the lumps are gone and they're light and fluffy.

5 Shape them into a hill on your plate, add remaining butter at the top, and enjoy watching the sunrise as it melts!

Milky Maple Soda

A heavenly "tree juice" soda, just like they serve in Ralph's Roofless Restaurant.

Ingredients *yields 1 serving*

- Milk (whole, low fat, or no fat)
- Plain seltzer
- 1 tablespoon maple syrup

YOU'LL BE SAP-HAPPY!

Directions

1 Fill ¼ of a glass with milk.

2 Fill the rest of the glass with seltzer, leaving a little room at the top.

3 Add about a tablespoon of maple syrup (more or less, to your taste).

4 Stir and slurp!

A refreshingly delicious twist on an old-fashioned bubbly beverage called an egg cream. No eggs. No cream.

40

A Lemony Blizzard

Grandpa will clear a path from your plate to your mouth!

Ingredients *yields 4 servings*

- ½ cup freshly squeezed lemon juice (3–4 lemons)
- ¾ cup granulated sugar
- 2 cups whole milk
- Dash of salt
- Sprinkles (optional)
- Whipped cream (optional)

IT'S THE WONDERFUL BLIZZARD OF AHHS!

Directions

1 In a metal bowl, whisk lemon juice, sugar, milk, and salt together. Cover the bowl.

2 Freeze for at least 4 hours, uncovering and whisking every 30 minutes to keep the mixture from freezing solid.

3 When ready for dessert, remove bowl from freezer and give the mixture a final whisking.

4 Scoop individual servings into bowls or glasses and top with sprinkles and snowy whipped cream if desired.

An edible blizzard in winter or summer!

Giant Chocolate Chip Cookie

Here's a huge pizza-size cookie that you can bake in your oven . . . in a pizza pan, of course. It's just like the one Grandpa brought back from his trip.

Ingredients *yields 10–12 servings*

- 1 cup sweet butter, softened, plus a little more for greasing pan
- ¾ cup dark brown sugar (tamp it down in measuring cup)
- ¾ cup granulated sugar
- 1 teaspoon vanilla extract
- 2 large eggs (room temperature works best)
- 2¼ cups all-purpose flour
- 1 teaspoon baking soda
- ¾ teaspoon salt
- 2½ cups semisweet chocolate chips

Directions

1 Preheat oven to 375 degrees.

2 In a very big bowl, beat butter (set aside a little bit for greasing the pan), sugars, and vanilla with a hand mixer until fluffy and light, about 2 to 3 minutes. Add the eggs, one at a time, beating well.

3 In a separate bowl, whisk together flour, baking soda, and salt. Add to butter mixture, a little at a time, beating until it's all blended together.

4 Stir in the best part—the chocolate chips.

5 Grease a round pizza pan lightly with butter. Pour dough in and spread out evenly with spatula.

6 Bake for 30 to 35 minutes.

7 Cool on a rack and slice with a pizza cutter!

Eat a slice!

HOLD THE PEPPERONI!

43

greetings from –
JELL-O STONE NATIONAL PARK

44

Jell-O Setting in the West

Cook up a wonderfully colorful, wiggly, and jiggly indoor sunset, right in your kitchen.

Ingredients *yields 8 servings*

- 1 3-ounce package of red Jell-O
- 1 3-ounce package of yellow Jell-O

UNBEARABLY DELICIOUS!

Directions

1 Pour each package of Jell-O into separate medium-size bowls and prepare according to package instructions.

2 Put both bowls into the refrigerator and keep checking *frequently*, with a spoon, to see when the Jell-O begins to set but is not firm—about 1 to 1½ hours. Jell-O should be like a *very* thick liquid.

3 Remove both bowls from the fridge. Gently spoon some of the red Jell-O into eight glass serving bowls. Then gently spoon some of the yellow Jell-O on top of the red. Repeat the process until you have two to four red and yellow layers of your sunset in each bowl. It doesn't matter whether the colors get mixed up a bit!

4 Refrigerate for at least 2 hours until firm.

Eat your sunset any time of day.

TALLCAKE TOWER

Strawberry Tallcake

Wouldn't you like to build a shortcake skyscraper and then eat it? Here's how you can do it.

Ingredients *yields 8 servings*

- 1 package yellow, store-bought shortcakes
- 1 pint strawberries, washed, hulled, and sliced
- 1 can whipped cream (light or low fat if preferred)

THE VIEW IS GREAT FROM UP HERE!

Directions

1 Put one shortcake on a large plate. This will be the bottom floor of your skyscraper. Fill it with a layer of sliced berries and then add some whipped cream. The cream will act as "cement" between the floors of your building and will help it stand up.

2 Add a second shortcake layer on top of the whipped cream, press it down gently, and layer it with strawberries. Then top it with whipped cream. Now you have a two-story building.

3 Continue to add more stories to your building by adding layer after layer of shortcakes and berries and whipped cream, until your skyscraper is tall and delicious looking. But beware, danger is lurking! How many stories do you think you can build before it topples over? Try to stop before it does.

4 But . . . if it topples, eat it anyway. It'll be a bit messy, but just as tasty.

Share your skyscraper with friends or family and you can all scrape your plates clean!

Grandpa's "Welcome Home" Cake

Bake and decorate a cake that looks like him. You can even eat his mustache and eyebrows.

Ingredients *yields 12 servings*

- 1 box cake mix, any flavor, plus ingredients listed on box
- 1 can frosting (you can make Grandpa any color you want)
- 1 tube red frosting (to decorate his face)
- 1 store-bought mini cupcake (for nose)
- 4 cookies (for eyes and ears)
- Shredded coconut (for hair)

I NEVER LOOKED SWEETER!

Directions

1 Follow directions on the cake mix box for a one-layer cake. (You should use a 9-inch round cake pan.) Let cake cool.

2 Remove cake from pan and put it on a plate larger than the cake itself. That leaves extra room for drips!

3 Frost cake all over top and around sides using a spatula. Make swirls for the cheeks and "draw" a smile into the frosting for the mouth.

4 Place the cupcake in the center for Grandpa's nose.

5 Squeeze the tube of frosting to create his eyebrows, mustache, eyeglasses, and smile. Mix frosting for cheeks.

6 Add cookies for his ears and eyes and coconut for his hair.

Glad you're home, Grandpa!

DEAR GRANDPA,

THANKS FOR GIVING US THESE CHEWANDSWALLOW RECIPES. WE'LL ALWAYS TREASURE THEM.

YOU'RE RIGHT ABOUT SATURDAY MORNING, PANCAKE MORNING. IT'S STILL OUR FAVORITE TIME OF THE WEEK, THANKS TO YOU!

NOW YOU'VE TAUGHT US HOW TO FLIP OUR OWN PANCAKES. AND NONE HAVE LANDED ON ANYONE'S HEAD.

THE RECIPES ARE AMAZING. IT'S BEEN FUN SHOPPING FOR THE INGREDIENTS WITH YOU... THEN CHOPPING THEM, STIRRING THEM, COOKING THEM, BAKING THEM, AND ESPECIALLY EATING THE TASTY RESULTS.

WE'VE DEFINITELY COOKED UP MANY A DELICIOUS STORM!

HUGS 'N' KISSES,
KATE AND HENRY

Index

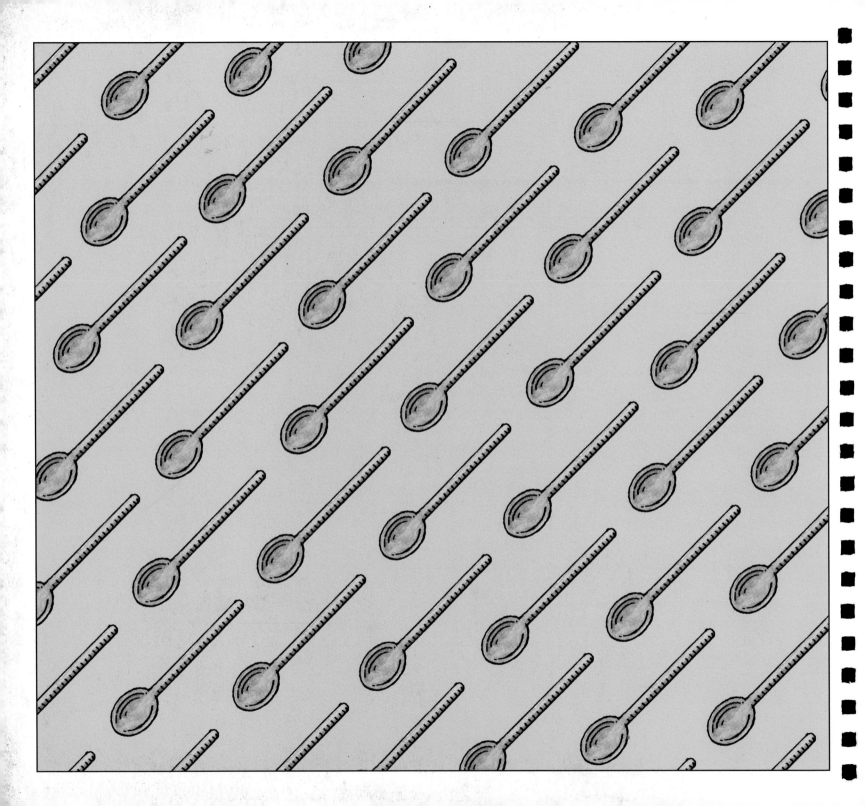